WHAT PET SHOULD I GET?

By Dr. Seuss

Random House 🏠 New York

August 2015

TM & copyright © by Dr. Seuss Enterprises, L.P. 2015

All rights reserved.
Published in the United States by Random House Children's Books,
a division of Penguin Random House LLC, New York.

Random House and the colophon are registered trademarks
of Penguin Random House LLC.

Back matter images in order of appearance:
Photographs of Ted Geisel and Theophrastus, and of Ted Geisel and Rex: collection of Margaretha Owens and Ted Owens;
photograph of Ted Geisel and Irish setter: Gene Lester/Archive Photos/Getty Images;
photograph of Ted and Helen Geisel with dog on beach: John Bryson/The LIFE Images Collection/Getty Images;
photograph of Ted Geisel and Yorkshire terrier: © William James Warren/Science Faction/Corbis;
black-and-white image from *What Pet Should I Get?*: TM & © by Dr. Seuss Enterprises, L.P. 2015;
black-and-white image from *One Fish Two Fish Red Fish Blue Fish*: TM & © by Dr. Seuss Enterprises, L.P. 1960, renewed 1988;
original, uncolorized spread from *What Pet Should I Get?*: TM & © by Dr. Seuss Enterprises, L.P. 2015;
colored pencil on photostat with acetate and tissue overlays for *I Can Read with My Eyes Shut!*: courtesy of Dr. Seuss Enterprises, L.P. 1978.

Visit us on the Web!
Seussville.com
randomhousekids.com

Educators and librarians, for a variety of teaching tools, visit us at RHTeachersLibrarians.com

Library of Congress Cataloging-in-Publication Data is available upon request.

ISBN 978-0-553-52426-0 (trade) — ISBN 978-0-553-52427-7 (lib. bdg.)

Printed in the United States of America   10 9 8 7 6 5 4 3 2 1   First Edition

PETS

We want a pet.
We want a pet.
What kind of pet
should we get?

Dad said we could have one.
Dad said he would pay.
I went to the Pet Shop.
I went there with Kay.

And so we went in . . .

I took one fast look . . .
I saw a fine dog who shook hands.
So we shook.

So I said,
"I want him!"

But then, Kay saw a cat.
She gave it a pat,
and she said, "I want THAT!"

Then Kay said, "Now what
do you think we should do?
Dad said to pick one.
We can not take home two."

Then what do you know?
We saw two other kinds.
NOW how could Kay and I
make up our minds?

A pup and a kitten.
They looked like good fun.
NOW which would we pick?
We could only pick one.

The cat?
Or the dog?
The kitten?
The pup?

Oh, boy!
It is something
to make a mind up.

Then I looked all around.
I saw something with wings.
I said, "Look at him!
We can pick one that sings."

But THEN . . .

"Look over there!"
said my sister Kay.
"We can go home
with a rabbit today!"

Then I looked at Kay.
I said, "What will we do?
I like all the pets that I see.
So do you.

We have to pick ONE pet
and pick it out soon.
You know Mother told us
to be back by noon."

And I could have done it.
I could have, I bet.
I could have said
what pet we should get.

BUT . . .

you know what Kay did . . .

Do you know what she did?

She said, "FISH!
          FISH!
            FISH!
              FISH!
It may be a fish
is the pet that we wish!"

THEN . . .

I saw a new kind!
And they were good, too!
How could I pick one?
Now what should we do?
We could only pick one.
That is what my dad said.
But how could I make up
that mind in my head?

Pick a pet fast!
Pick one out soon!

Mother and Dad said
to be home by noon!

The time may be now
to make up my mind.
But who knows what other
good pets I might find?

I might find a new one.
A fast kind of thing
who would fly round my head
in a ring on a string!

Yes, that would be fun . . .

BUT . . .

our house is so small.
This thing on a string
would bump, bump into the wall!
My mother, I know,
would not like that at all.

SO, maybe some other
good kind of pet.
Another kind maybe
is what we should get.

We might find a new kind.
A pet who is tall.
A tall pet who fits
in a space that is small.

My mother might like
this pet best of them all.

If we had a big tent,
then we would be able
to take home a YENT!
Dad would like us
to have a good YENT.
BUT, how do I know
he would pay for a tent?

So, you see how it is
when you pick out a pet.
How can you make up
your mind what to get?

BUT . . .

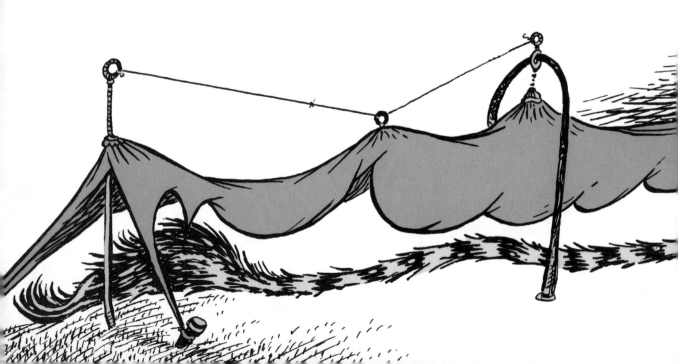

What if we took
one of each kind of pet?
Then our house would be full
of the pets we would get.

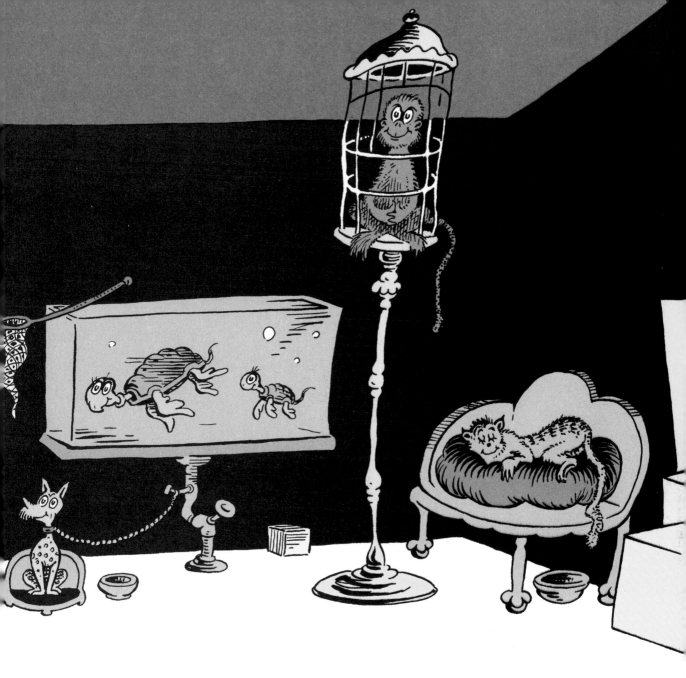

NO . . .

Dad would be mad.
We can only have one.
If we do not choose,
we will end up with **NONE**.

"I will do it right now.
I will do it!" I said.
"I will make up the mind
that is up in my head."

The dog . . . ? Or the rabbit . . . ?
The fish . . . ? Or the cat . . . ?
I picked one out fast,
and then that was that.

WHAT PET SHOULD I GET?

NOTES FROM THE PUBLISHER

In *Happy Birthday to You!*, Dr. Seuss writes:

> A Present! A-*ha!*
> Now what kind shall I give . . . ?
> Why, the kind you'll remember
> As long as you live!

And the present he suggests? A "fine pet."

Dr. Seuss was an animal lover. His work is filled with creatures of all kinds, and he kept and cared for animals throughout his life. He is famous for one Cat in particular—but when choosing a pet, he seems to have favored dogs.

At Random House, we also love animals. In fact, many of us are crazy about them, and we celebrate them in our personal lives and in the books we publish.

Pets are life-changing. They greet us like heroes when we walk in the door, comfort us when we are sad, and love us unconditionally. Dogs and cats are the most popular pets in the United States, but these wonderful, vulnerable animals can easily live for over a decade and are dependent on us for all their needs. So committing to caring for a pet as a cherished, not captive, companion is a big decision.

Choosing *where* to get your pet is also very important. When Dr. Seuss wrote *What Pet Should I Get?* over fifty years ago, it was common for people to simply buy dogs, cats, and other animals at pet stores. Today animal advocates encourage us to adopt them from a shelter or rescue organization and warn us never to purchase our pets from places that are supplied by puppy mills. We wholeheartedly agree and completely support this recommendation. Choosing to adopt can help save the life of an animal that may not otherwise get a second chance at finding a forever home. Did you know that you can rescue all kinds of animals, including birds, turtles, rabbits, and guinea pigs?

Many organizations have easy-to-find information about adoption, shelter locations, and animal-care tips, as well as how to help at-risk animals in your community. This is a responsibility all of us share.

Dr. Seuss's first "pet" was a brown stuffed toy dog given to him by his mother. Ted—whose real name was Theodor Seuss Geisel—named it Theophrastus. Ted would keep Theophrastus for the rest of his life. The dog was often perched near his drawing board. In 1991, just days before his death at the age of eighty-seven, Ted gave Theophrastus to his stepdaughter Lea Grey. "You will take care of the dog, won't you?" he asked her.

Around 1914, when Ted was ten years old, he had a real *live* dog—a Boston bulldog named Rex. Rex had a habit of walking on three of his four feet. Perhaps this is where Ted's ideas for odd-legged animals came from?

(Left) Six-year-old Ted walks his toy dog Theophrastus on a leash, circa 1910.

(Below) Ted and his dog Rex in Springfield, Massachusetts, circa 1914.

Ted and his dog Cluny review proofs beside the swimming pool at home in La Jolla, California, 1957.

On a beach near their California home, Ted draws in the sand while his wife Helen and Cluny observe, 1959.

Ted and his wife Helen had an Irish setter named Cluny. Ted's neighbor in La Jolla, California, had bred Irish setters, and according to Ted's biographers Judith and Neil Morgan, "a succession of them [were] a constant in the Geisels' life." Once, when Helen was ill, Ted set up a series of mirrors so that she could be comforted by the sight of Cluny waiting outside her hospital window.

After Helen's death in 1967, Ted remarried. Ted and Helen had liked big dogs. His second wife, Audrey, preferred small dogs. They acquired a miniature Yorkshire terrier named Sam (short for Samantha). It was their first of many Yorkies over the years.

Ted and his dog Sam at home in La Jolla in 1979. Behind them is one of Ted's creations—a Semi-Normal Green-Lidded Fawn.

Despite his love of dogs, it was a Cat that had the biggest influence on Ted's career. In the spring of 1957, Random House published his thirteenth children's book, *The Cat in the Hat*. It was an instant critical and commercial success. Ted— who had been writing for twenty years—was an "overnight" sensation! More changes came quickly. Within months, he became president of a new division of Random House called Beginner Books—a publishing house within a publishing house that specialized in books aimed at beginning readers, like *The Cat in the Hat*. Then, in the fall of 1957, Random House would publish Ted's book *How the Grinch Stole Christmas!* Like *Cat,* it was a blockbuster hit. "Dr. Seuss" was a bona fide celebrity!

From 1958 through 1962, Ted was very busy. He edited twenty-three Beginner Books by other authors. He set up a sculpting studio and designed a line of Dr. Seuss toys with interchangeable body parts. And he wrote eight new children's books: *Yertle the Turtle and Other Stories* (1958), *The Cat in the Hat Comes Back* (1958), *Happy Birthday to You!* (1959), *One Fish Two Fish Red Fish Blue Fish* (1960), *Green Eggs and Ham* (1960), *The Sneetches and Other Stories* (1961), *Ten Apples Up*

On Top! (1961, written under his pseudonym Theo. LeSieg—Geisel spelled backward), and *Dr. Seuss's Sleep Book* (1962).

Shortly after Ted's death in 1991, his wife Audrey found a box of materials for various projects in his studio. She set it aside with other things of Ted's. The box was rediscovered by Audrey and Claudia Prescott—Ted Geisel's longtime secretary and friend—in the fall of 2013. Among the contents were the manuscript and finished line art for what would become *What Pet Should I Get?*

According to Audrey, "While undeniably special, it is not surprising to me that we found this because Ted always worked on multiple projects and started new things all the time—he was constantly writing and drawing and coming up with ideas for new stories." It was perfectly normal for him to start something, then put it away to work on later.

Cathy Goldsmith was Ted's art director at Random House for the last eleven years of his life. When Cathy first saw the *Pet* artwork, she felt certain that it dated to the period between 1958 and 1962. She recognized that the children in *Pet* are the same as the kids in *One Fish Two Fish Red Fish Blue Fish!*

There is no real plot to *One Fish Two Fish Red Fish Blue Fish.* In it, we meet a boy and girl who appear to be brother and sister. They introduce the reader to a group of funny fish, then to more and more

(Left) The kids from *What Pet Should I Get?*

(Below) The kids from *One Fish Two Fish Red Fish Blue Fish.*

fantastical creatures—many of which they keep as pets. Could Ted's idea for *What Pet Should I Get?* have evolved into *One Fish Two Fish Red Fish Blue Fish?* We'll never know for sure.

But we do know that throughout his career, Ted recycled parts of stories he wrote to use in new stories. For example, a story he wrote for *Redbook* magazine in 1951 called "The Strange Shirt Spot" featured a gooey green stain that gets transferred from one object to another. Ted reused the stubborn stain (this time in pink) in *The Cat in the Hat Comes Back,* published in 1958.

Ted Geisel was a perfectionist. He could spend months developing a character, days talking about the placement of a comma. "I know my stuff looks like it was rattled off in twenty-eight seconds," he said, "but every word is a struggle and every sentence is like the pangs of birth." Ted once estimated that for a typical sixty-four-page book, he would produce over a thousand pages of text and images. He revised his text over and over and over again.

Like other Ted projects, the pages Audrey found for *What Pet Should I Get?* had text taped into position on the original line art. Multiple versions of the text were placed on top of each other.

A spread from *What Pet Should I Get?* as it was originally found, with text taped into position.

In some places, it was unclear which revisions were the most recent. In a few places, words were missing or too faint to see. Like Kay and her brother, the editors at Random House had to make decisions and stick with them. We thought very carefully about each one, and we hope Dr. Seuss would be pleased—and that you will be, too.

Once the text was final, it was time to add color to the artwork. With the exception of a few books (like *Happy Birthday to You!*) that were painted in full color, Ted usually delivered black-line art, along with a set of copies on which he indicated where the color went. In the example below, Ted used colored pencils to show the colors he wanted for a spread from *I Can Read with My Eyes Shut!* The numbers refer to colors on a custom chart created especially for Ted to use when choosing his colors.

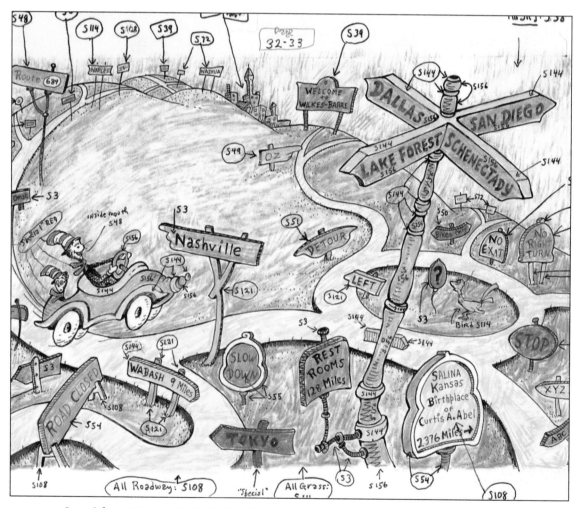

Spread from *I Can Read with My Eyes Shut!*, marked by Ted with numbers to indicate colors.

Only a few color indications were found with the *Pet* art, so Art Director Cathy Goldsmith had to make a lot of decisions. Because she thought the book was so closely related to *One Fish,* she used the color palette of that book as her starting point. The interior of *One Fish* prints in four special inks. We'll call them blue, red, yellow, and black. In no place in *One Fish* are the inks mixed to create another color. There is no green, no purple, no orange, no brown. Most of the books that Ted wrote before 1963 are characterized by this limited color palette. After 1963, however, Ted's books—and picture books in general—have a fuller color palette created by mixing colors. For *Pet,* Cathy chose to colorize the book in a way that bridges the gap between the limited color palette of *One Fish* and the more fully colored books like *Hop on Pop.* She colored all the backgrounds and objects in *Pet* blue or red or yellow or black. Mixed inks were used to create the colors of the real-life pets as well as the children's hair and skin tone.

What Pet Should I Get? is a story about a classic childhood moment: choosing a pet. It is also a story about making decisions—sometimes it's hard, but you just have to make up your mind. In fact, by ending the story the way he did, Dr. Seuss encourages readers to make up their own minds about how the story ends.

So what do *you* think? What kind of pet *did* the kids get?